TO BE A DRUM

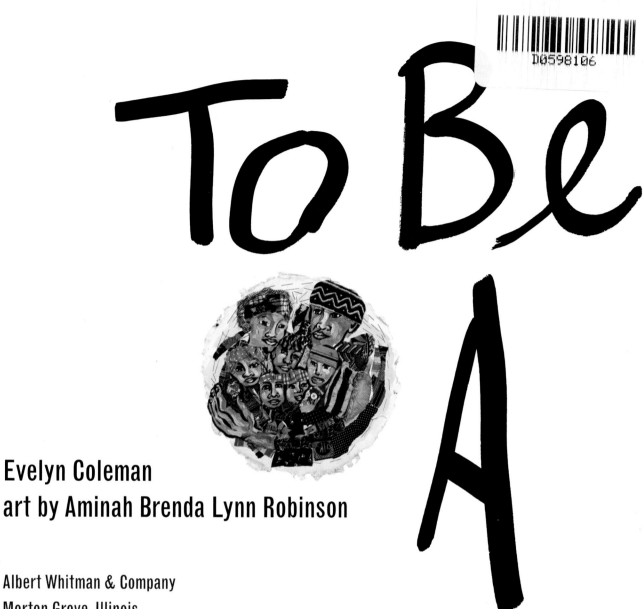

Evelyn Coleman
art by Aminah Brenda Lynn Robinson

Albert Whitman & Company
Morton Grove, Illinois

Also by Evelyn Coleman:

White Socks Only
The Riches of Oseola McCarty

Library of Congress Cataloging-in-Publication Data

Coleman, Evelyn, 1948-

To be a drum / written by Evelyn Coleman;

illustrated by Aminah Brenda Lynn Robinson.

p. cm.

Summary: Daddy Wes tells how Africans were brought to America
as slaves, but promises his children that as long as they can hear
the rhythm of the earth, they will be free.

ISBN 0-8075-8006-6 (hardcover)

ISBN 0-8075-8007-4 (paperback)

[1. Afro-Americans——Fiction. 2. Slavery——Fiction. 3. Drum——Fiction.]

I. Robinson, Aminah Brenda Lynn, ill. II. Title.

PZ7.C6746To 1997

[E]——dc21

96-54068

CIP AC

Published in 1998 by Albert Whitman & Company,

6340 Oakton Street, Morton Grove, Illinois 60053-2723.

Published simultaneously in Canada by General Publishing,

Limited, Toronto.
Printed in the United States of America.

10 9 8 7 6 5 4 3

The design is by Scott Piehl.

To my granddaughter, Taylor Blayne Parker:
May your drum forever beat.
And to all the children of the world: Be a drum.
—E.C.

To the memories of my mother and great-aunt:
Helen Elizabeth Zimmerman Robinson (1916-1995)
and Cornelia Johnson (1852-1957) who passed it on.

To my sisters, Sandra Sue Robinson Scott and
Sarah Elizabeth Robinson Barnes, and to their
families, with love.
—A.B.L.R.

The illustrations were created using homemade
dyes and paper and incorporating pieces of cloth
and various other materials, including wool and
sisal threads from Kenya, clay, sand, wood strips,
raw cotton, vintage buttons, and basket fragments.

Some of the cloth scraps were taken from a quilt
made by the artist's great-aunt when she was a
slave in Georgia. Other scraps were collected from
clothing dating from the early twentieth century
to the present.

When I was a child, my father taught me that all people are connected by the earth's heartbeat, a part of the spirit that allows our existence. He directed me to put my ear to the bare earth and to listen. I did hear a heartbeat—perhaps my own, perhaps the earth's. This story grew from such times during my childhood.

Seeing my message envisioned through color and form was a profound and joyful experience for me. I cannot faithfully put it into words, except to say that Aminah Robinson's art sounds in my spirit like a drum.

Evelyn Coleman

When I first read Evelyn Coleman's manuscript, I was touched deeply. I was transported to a past, present, and future that blended together like the sound of beating drums. I saw Africa, the Middle Passage, slavery, the civil-rights struggle, black artists, teachers, and heroes, and, always, the children, looking toward tomorrow. I knew that the art must be transformative. And I knew that I had found my sister in spirit.

Aminah Brenda Lynn Robinson

During a morning mist, the fog swirled up around Mat, Martha, and their daddy. And when they sat cross-legged, they couldn't be seen from afar. But they were there.

Then Daddy Wes told them a story in his soft voice, the voice that could tap, tap, tap Mat and Martha gently on their hearts.

Daddy Wes began. "Long before time, before hours and minutes and seconds, on the continent of Africa, the rhythm of the earth beat for the first people.

The earth filled the air with spirit.

The spirit rose on the wind and flew into our bodies. And our own hearts beat for the first time. We were alive!

The beat moved through our bodies and pushed out from our fingers.

That is how our drum was born.

With the drum we spoke to the animals and to the people.

The earth's heart beat out the rhythm of all there is. We listened—

and sounded the rhythms back for her to hear.

Then men from another continent came—
men who would not listen to the rhythm of the earth.
They shackled us, the people of the earth's color,
and flung us into the bellies of ships, bringing
us enslaved across the oceans and the seas.

They tore us apart from one another and did
not allow us to speak our own languages.
We were a lost people. We were no longer free.
We thought we were no more.
Then they took the drums away.

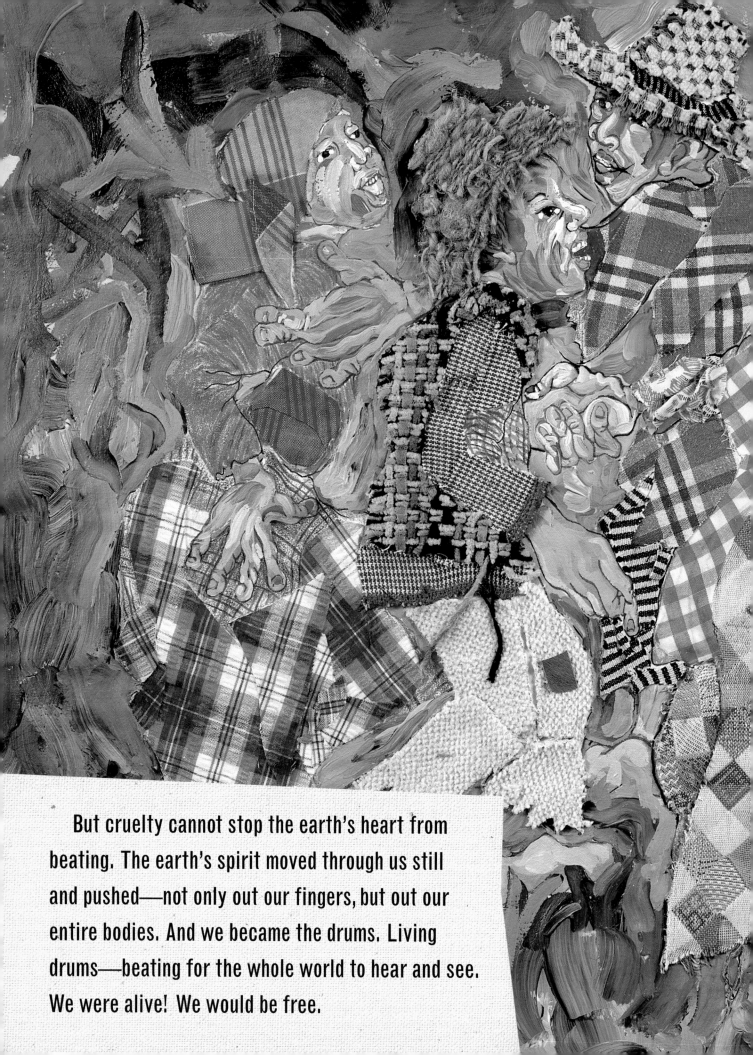

But cruelty cannot stop the earth's heart from beating. The earth's spirit moved through us still and pushed—not only out our fingers, but out our entire bodies. And we became the drums. Living drums—beating for the whole world to hear and see. We were alive! We would be free.

So when we worked in the fields,
we made our feet drums.

When we sang songs under starlit
skies, we made our mouths drums.

When we talked to each other,
we made our speech drums.

When we stitched our quilts,
we made our hands drums.

When we fought in wars, we made our courage drums.

When we invented things, we made our minds drums.

When we fought for our freedom and for our civil rights, we made our communities drums.

When we created music, paintings, sculpture, dances, and dramas, we made our art drums.

When we wrote down our wisdom, we made our stories drums.

When we recorded our memories, we made our history drums.

When we became farmers, scientists, teachers, leaders, entrepreneurs, and tradespeople, we made our dreams drums.

We were the earth's people. We were the living drums.

We would always be free."

Daddy Wes leaned over and whispered, "Listen, do you hear?" He stretched out on the earth, his arms spread like a bird's wings.

Mat and Martha lay down close beside and put their ears to the ground, too.

They waited for the magic to be theirs. Waited for the hearing of the earth's heartbeat. Waited to *become*.

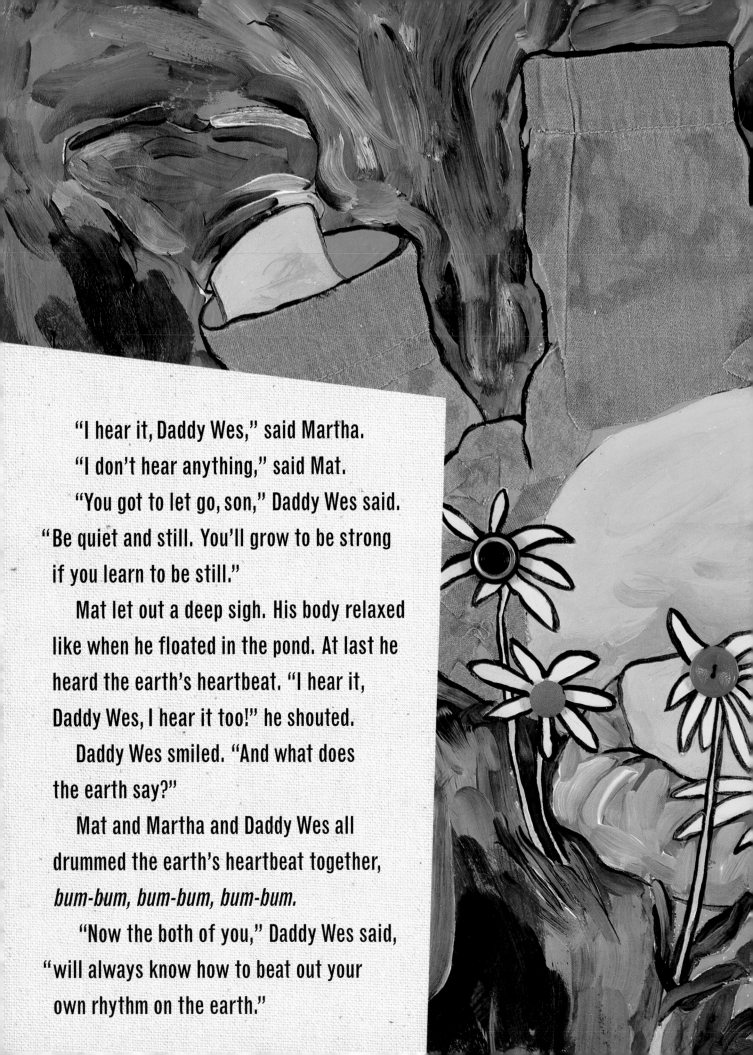

"I hear it, Daddy Wes," said Martha.

"I don't hear anything," said Mat.

"You got to let go, son," Daddy Wes said. "Be quiet and still. You'll grow to be strong if you learn to be still."

Mat let out a deep sigh. His body relaxed like when he floated in the pond. At last he heard the earth's heartbeat. "I hear it, Daddy Wes, I hear it too!" he shouted.

Daddy Wes smiled. "And what does the earth say?"

Mat and Martha and Daddy Wes all drummed the earth's heartbeat together, *bum-bum, bum-bum, bum-bum.*

"Now the both of you," Daddy Wes said, "will always know how to beat out your own rhythm on the earth."

Then Daddy Wes, Mat, and Martha took each other's hands and strolled from the field with the heartbeat of the earth sounding their way.

You, too, can be free.

Become a drum.